Love is in the morning when you wake and smile at me.

Love is when we talk together,

happy as can be.

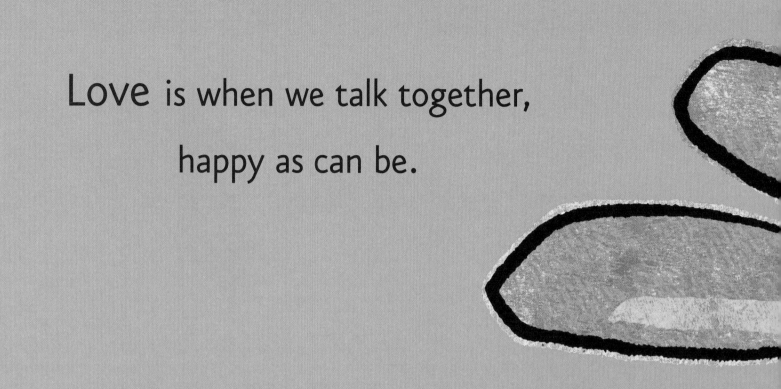

Sometimes love is quiet
and it needs no words at all.

Love is there
to catch you
when you are
about to fall.

Love is when we huddle close
and shelter from a shower.

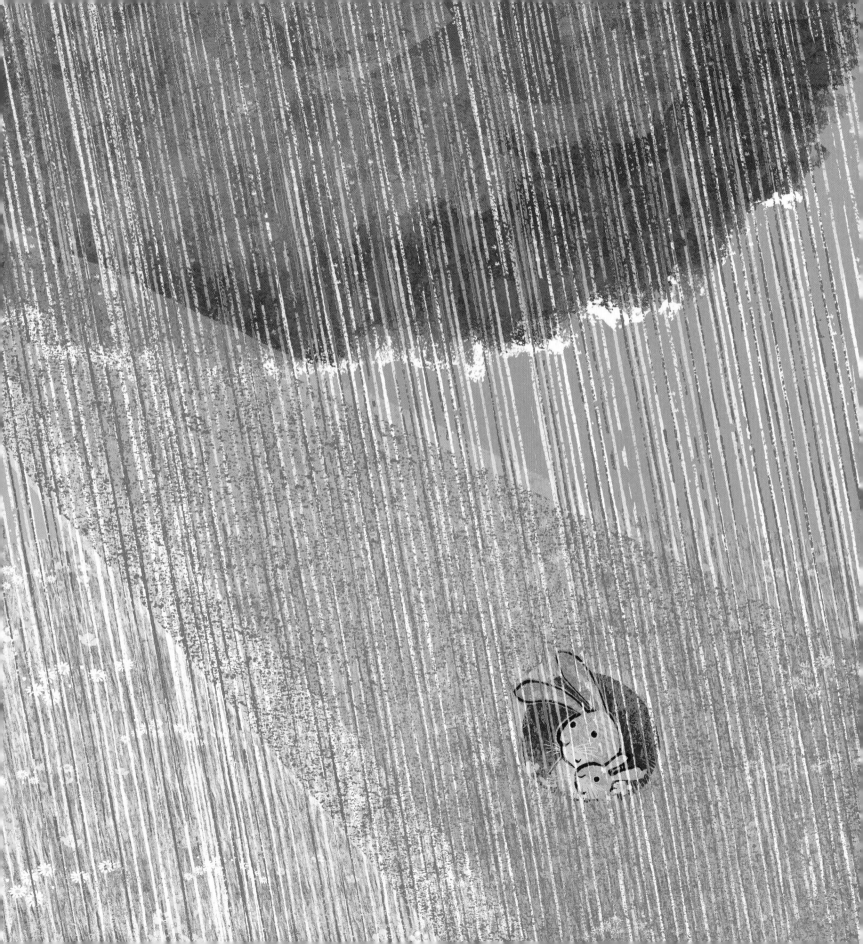

Love is when

we take the

time to stop and

smell a flower.

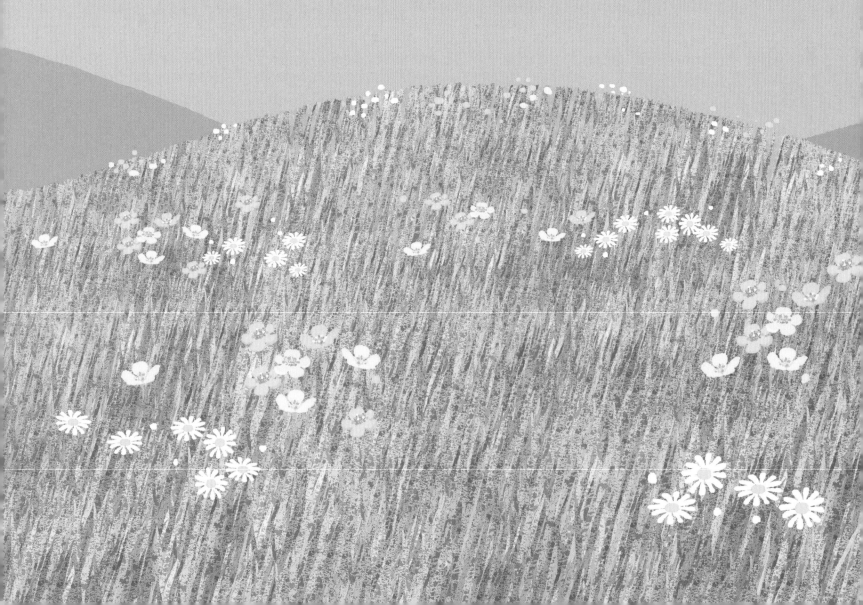

I love you when you get it right,
and when you get it wrong.

The world is
much more lovely
since the day you
came along.

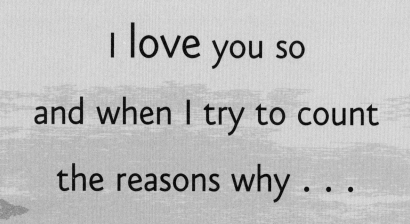

I love you so
and when I try to count
the reasons why . . .

. . . I find there are more reasons . . .

. . . than there are

stars in the sky.

First published 2015 by Nosy Crow Ltd
The Crow's Nest, 10a Lant Street
London SE1 1QR
www.nosycrow.com

This edition published 2017

ISBN 978 0 85763 931 8 (PB)

A CIP catalogue record for this book is available from the British Library.

Printed in China by Imago
Papers used by Nosy Crow are made from
wood grown in sustainable forests.

1 3 5 7 9 8 6 4 2 (PB)